GW00374708

T.M. Cooks is the pen name of the following collaborative writing team. The contributors are:

- Eve Irving

- Victoria Kaczmarczyk

- Amy Parker

- Korbyn Wood

- Charlotte Cooke

- Morgan Davidson

- Jacob Cliffe

- Kyla Gater

with cover design by Wren Jones (froggyfroo-art.carrd.co). The project was overseen by Joe Reddington.

The group cheerfully acknowledges the wonderful help given by:

- Joanna Rankin

- Emma Johnson

- Alison E. Johnson

- Everyone in the English department

- and special thanks goes to 'Many Pretty Blankets'.

And a big thank you goes to Higher Horizons who funded this wonderful project.

It's been a wonderful opportunity, and everyone involved has been filled with incredible knowledge and enthusiasm.

Finally, we would like to thank all staff at Sir William Stanier School for their support in releasing our novelists from lessons for a full week.

The group started to plan out their novel at 9.15 on Monday 4th October 2021 and completed their last proofreading at 13.20 on Friday 8th October 2021.

We are incredibly proud to state that every word of the story, every idea, every chapter and yes, every mistake, is entirely their own work. No teachers, parents or other students touched a single key during this process, and we would ask readers to keep this in mind.

We are sure you will agree that this is an incredible achievement. It has been a true delight and privilege to see this group of young people turn into professional novelists in front of our very eyes.

The System

T. M. Cooks

Contents

Chapter 1

One Bad Day

In his office, Bruce, the warden of the prison, was having a miserable day. He glanced out of the window, the weather disgusting and pouring down with rain. It was gloomy and dark, making his mood even worse. Bruce was a short man but had a very muscular body, tattoos showered up his arms and his royal blue eyes gleamed with boredom. Bruce was a lonely man with no wife or children and spent all of his days in his office sulking about life in general. He barely had any affection shown towards him and wasn't the best towards giving it either due to the lack of experience. Bruce liked the system and the way everything was segregated; this would make Bruce's day a little brighter in his mind which was almost always full of darkness.

Not knowing what to do, Bruce gets up and goes for his daily prison check. Shaking with fear and mortified to walk past that one cell, he sucked it up and portrayed like he wasn't scared one bit. One of the guards was also looking around making sure nothing had happened. The warden and the guard made eye contact. Acting like they don't know each other, they walked off and casually carried on with their day.

Len was the kind of prisoner you should be scared of, he was very tall and skinny, he looked frozen cold inside and out. His soul was sucked out and there was just an empty human shell left behind. Every guard that would pass by would shake uncontrollably with fear although you would think it'd be the other way around, it definitely wasn't. The warden was fed up with the inmates being all forte, he built his anger up and finally let it all out. The room quietened. The hallways went silent. The System stopped. The inmates finally listened to Bruce and gave in. He was shocked. With his confidence high, Bruce headed to the protest, his mindset to stop whatever was taking place.

Chapter 2

The Protest That Started It All

Pro green protests were happening everywhere. Both blue and green supremacists were getting violent at these protests, people scared for their lives had to run as far as they could away from this. As you walked around this protest all you could see was people fighting and guns being fired. Not being able to actually hear them, since all greens are mute, you could hear them in your head. The voice being loud, not being able to make it stop. There was one old couple that stood out to everyone. Why were they here? An old couple shouldn't be risking it like this. The old man's name was Walter, he was 57, he was short with grey hair and green eyes, he walked off with one of his friends. Not knowing what would happen he left his wife alone thinking it would be okay. Gunshots were fired. Everyone screamed. What had happened?

Walter, not thinking much of it, casually heads back to his wife. He couldn't find her. Where was she? Walter walks around looking for her. He stumbled upon a body. It was her. She had been shot. Walter tried to signal for help, everyone ignoring him. Faces pacing past him, pushing, barging, flashing lights piercing the highstreet, Walter life crumbled before his eyes his one true love, his wife lying lifeless in his cold arms, her face soulless, a single tear rolls down his wrinkled face as his world has just ended in the matter of a second.

The police showed up, jumping out of their vehicles, armed and very stern. Most of the greens had run off, hidden in the dark corners of the buildings. However, Walter was still there. He couldn't believe

his wife was gone, he felt empty and helpless. Whilst he was crying over the body
of his wife, the police had already seen
him. The police grabbed him, threw him
into the back of a big caged van with cold
metal touching his skin as he lay powerless
on the floor of the van, since he's a green.
Walter had been taken into prison. Still
crying, he's not understanding what's actually going on. He got put in a cell with
Len, Len did not seem too happy about
being together. He liked to be alone, not
with some old man. Bruce seemed off, normally he'd already shouted at the inmates,
but today he went straight back to his office. What was up with him? The inmates
all wondered.

Chapter 3

The Silent Session

At the prison, which was a huge dull

building in a remote part of the kingdom, it was so remote that the only transport to get there were the underground trucks which only the special forces knew the location of. The security was ridiculously high and no one even dared to step a foot close to the prison because of this. Newly added greens were being added to their cells from the recent protest which was shut down. A therapist, Eva Marshal, was brought to help an inmate as he had hallucinated from his recent episode. Eva hated the job she was selected for but being blue, she had no choice. Eva didn't like how the system worked and the injustice on the greens. Greens were selected as they were lower in society, less money, and their jobs where selected as the low paid jobs. However blues had two different categories, light blue and royal blue. The light blues were the upper working class and the royal blues were the wealthy business category in society. These were all hand picked by the reds which were the royals. There was one more colour in society: yellows which are disabled or people with mental health. Yellows tend to be slaves to the reds as they have no other opportunities and don't get to pick what they can do.

People are differentiated by their eye colour, this shows the category that they are within.

Eva walked into the empty hallways of the prison, the walls as grey as dishwater and the floors as dull as a blunt knife. The heavy metal doors opened and then slammed as Eva rushed to her appointment. The guards were yelling on the tanoi for Leonard Bullock to go to the therapy room. Eva assumed this was her client. She went into the room and there sat two chairs with a tall lanky man slouched down, sinking into the chair. He had bright orange hair and bold green eyes. Eva was nervous but sat down to begin her session professionally.

"Hello, my name is Eva Marshall. I will be assisting you and we will be starting with some basic questions, shall we begin?"

Len didn't reply but in fact grunted as a somewhat response .

"So why are you here today, if you mind me asking?"

This man obviously couldn't respond, no words surfacing at all.

"I know this might be a scary experience for you Leonard but please try to speak." His face changed sullenly as if his jaw were locked. Couldn't he speak or was he just giving me a hard time?

Eva was confused and wondered why he was silenced. She went to go and ask a guard why the people with green eyes weren't speaking and he replied considerately.

"The greens were born mute."

"What? So how am I meant to help him if he can't talk to my patient?" Eva asked frustratedly.

"I can't do this, this isn't right, my job is to help and I can't help if I can't communicate."

Eva started feeling eager and exasperated, like someone was inside her head, under the pressure of her own mind. She wraps up the session, saying it's over. Eva speedly makes her way out of the tedious assignment of doors and gates to get out of the prison cell. Len sat stiff in his chair confused about what just happened because to his own knowledge there was still half an hour left. What did he do? Did she know? Eva gets stopped. The guard refuses to let her out of the cell. Eva explains her situation and says she needs a break. Sleep deprived nightmares. "Please I will stay if you just let me out!" she pleaded. He gave in and decided to let her go. Eva was relieved and never wanted to go back to that prison again.

Chapter 4

Undeniable Truth

Walter was sitting in his dirty little cell,

on his dusty bunk. He was daydreaming of his beloved long lost wife Lily. He dreamed of their wedding, the day trips with his wife and the baking for her return. But he couldn't do that anymore, he couldn't even make it through life without her by his side. Depression filled his yearning heart as flashbacks took over his mind: the church bells ringing, orchestra playing and a handsome groom awaiting a majestical and up beat wife to be wed. Feeling overwhelmed with the sorrow absorbing, he jumped back into his sad, sad reality. The reality of being half of a whole. The guards opened his cell "Breakfast" they grunt. Walter stood steadily and walked out through the door and down the long winding corridor to the cafeteria. He grabbed a tray and lined up in the queue with his cell pal, Len. Walter got the usual but he was too miserable to even eat so he took a seat and watched the time fly as his food went cold.

Whispers spoken aloud reveal an undeniable truth. Truth of the past. Truth that could kill ...who murdered Lily? Lily's murder was along side him throughout his journey, every waking hour of every waking day. He said nothing, he physically couldn't. Bruce murdered Lily. Bruce murdered Walter's soulmate. A range of emotions overcame him, leaving him unsure of how to act upon this. Ten years ago today Bruce killed his darling wife because she wanted rights for all. This was so unfair. They hated each other already but this! This left Walter with more than just hatred for Bruce. He loathed him and every-

thing about him. If he thought that Lily
didn't deserve to live then maybe neither
should he. An eye for an eye, tooth for a
tooth, life for a life. What is the worst that
could happen? He's in prison anyway.

Pete, Walter and Len caught first glances
as they met and exchanged looks. The un-
certainty rises as Walter is on edge.Pete
was a guard, not as scary as some but he
was scary in other ways. He had this aura
but it may as well just be the defensive
walls put up by inmates such as himself.
Pete was a very large and skinny man with
dirty blonde hair gelled down to his scalp.
He wore a guard's uniform and a tragic,
expressive face, this was because he was
always alone and lived in an awfully mea-
ger, desolate flat with his only companion,
a tree frog named Broccoli, who was Pete's

pride and joy.The one thing he lived for.

The thoughts of Pete's mind rang throughout Len and Walter's ears.Racing through the maze of their minds. How is this possible? Pete doesn't behold the power of greens because he's a wretched blue and he certainly couldn't possibly be both, that's preposterous. Walter and Len, now watched Pete trembling, frightened of who stood before them.The pair exchanged thoughts simultaneously and telepathically."Len do you think he is a green and blue combined?" "Walter, do you think he is green and blue combined?" Pete, being completely unaware and clueless, stood helplessly and blankly beside them as the others were dumbfounded, fearing for the day when Pete and the population would discover this revelation of a hybrid.

Chapter 5

The King's Message

King Leonard, otherwise known as Leo,

is a red which keeps him protected and safekept, hidden within his palace. He rules the kingdom and makes all resolutions in the system. His sidekick, Frederick, convinces the king to be occupied in the kingdom and guards a lot of secrets from Leo. Him being known as "The clueless king, " conveys that he doesn't know anything about the system or what the system was. Leo has only one son called Rupert, who was 19 years old and he was also oblivious about the system. Rupert has short and almost sutty coloured hair with a clean shaven face. He was tall and has a very masculine figure.

Frederick creates a speech for Leo addressing the recent riotous outburst of the green population but the king was nervous and anxious since he didn't really get informed about this. He never does. Frederich always oversteps him as if he was king and Leo wasn't really fair to him.Leo gets pushed to the sidelines every single time.

Leo neurotically prepared for the speech, applying his best sunday suit jacket onto his bold body, "Fredrick, are you sure this won't cause any uproar?" The king exaggerated to Frederick and he replied controllingly, "No, my lord, I strategically wrote this letter to make sure everyone was included." But deep down Frederich knew that SOMETHING could happen as most people might not appreciate it.

Leo steps onto the stage with a vast ocean of colours in the audience patiently waiting for the king's outlook on the green protest. Leo stuttered during his speech and unsure on what he's going to say has the greens infuriated, wanting a leader who can speak fairly on an important topic in the system, but him being as oblivious as always causes an uprising in society.

A few citizens consent with the speech but a lot of the percentage don't. The greens are unsettled by how biased the king is with his lack of knowledge. The royal blue's consent as the whole system is set up so they can have a better life and they can live freely with money but this means that the other colours have to remain distraught.

The guards are keeping a watch of the crowd as they can see the agitation and tension rising. The greens now shouting out of anger to the king, blurting out slurs and demanding equality. A royal blue clamors a rude comment about a green and this causes all the greens to have a turmoil.

A fight breaks out between royal blues and emerald greens; the king feels helpless and storms off the stage in embarrassment. Frederick seeks comfort for him as he's very distressed about how the greens viewed his presentation and how he's caused this outbreak in chaos.

Chapter 6

The Words Not 'Spoken'

It was night and the entire prison was

cold and damp. The only sound was the wind howling. Despite this, both Walter and Len were wide awake looking as though they were daydreaming but were actually having a conversation with their minds.

"So how has your day been Walter? Mine has been rubbish."

"Same old, I suppose."

As this was going on, Pete was doing his night patrol before he could return home and he was walking in complete silence until he passed their cell and once he did he overheard their conversation. This left Pete completely confused, he had no idea where the noise was coming from. He was alone in the hall and if the noise had come from the cell then who did it come from? He thought he must be hearing things as the prisoners were believed to be mute and this had been proven, or so he thought.

This confused Pete as he went home for the night and thought about how it is possible to hear the greens when they are mute. He then remembered where he had heard the noise, it was outside the prisoners he had met a couple of days prior, Walter and Len. This made some sense to Pete as when they had met they acted rather suspicious. Pete also noticed that when he was talking to them they were quiet but seemed to be listening to each other and not paying him much attention. Pete just thought that they were delusional and not writing in the head but now he was beginning to think that something else was going on. Pete eventually realised that they and potentially all the other prisoners were telepaths.

Despite his new discovery, Pete was still confused on how he could hear the greens as he was a blue. He speculated that because he has a green father that he could have potentially inherited some green traits but that was unheard of. But Pete couldn't stop thinking about whether or not it could be true. This thought stayed with Pete for a couple of days and he couldn't ask anyone for help because if anyone found out that he could potentially have green properties he would be punished immediately. However, he knew that the only logical answer is that he was a telepath.

Pete then realised something crucial, he had always thought that because his father was a green that he had some green blood in him this was proven to him by his one green eye that he was forced to cover up with a blue contact identical to his blue eye to make sure that he was

never discovered or bullied for it. But now that he had discovered the green's secret of telepathy

he realised he had inherited a lot more than a different coloured eye.

Still a bit confused, Pete goes to see Len and Walter to get some confirmation for his theories. When he made it to their cell, he stomped to get their attention. They popped up and Pete noticed that Len's face turned red immediately, Pete had clearly annoyed him.

"I know about your secret, about you and the other greens being telepaths, I know this because I overheard your conversation the other day and it confused me so I put two and two together and discovered that you're both telepathics and I think that I am one too."

"That is intriguing! I have to admit I have never heard of something like this."

This shocked Pete as he got an echo of Len's voice in his head. It was shattering loud but he tried with his might to connect to Len's mind so he could speak without opening his mouth but he struggled. So Pete just spoke normally. "If you can help me learn how to do what you do I will owe you a favour, anything you want."

This intrigued Len and suddenly Pete heard his voice again.

"Fine, I will help you." Pete was relieved and from that day, he began to practice.

Chapter 7

Envious Bonding

As Pete and Len talked more and more about Pete's unusual circumstances regarding that he is a blue yet has the properties of a green, they began to bond and Pete began to learn and get better with his telepathy. "It's fascinating, so your mum was a blue who fell in love with one of us greens, " said Len with a bit of aggressiveness in his words. "I still can't believe it to be honest, I hate my job even more now I see how they treat these greens, it's horrid and i know I'm also a blue but knowing this place and the stupid rules that it has, if anybody found out I'll be a goner."

With that Pete and Len ended their conversation as Pete's head was beginning to hurt . He goes back to his grimy flat and gets changed into some old clothes and checks on his pet frog, Broccoli. After doing his list of chores, he sits down and eats his favourite meal, barbeque noodles.

The next day, Pete is doing his usual

jobs at the prison, checking and guarding the prisoners, when all of a sudden he hears Len's voice and they have another conversation. Although very obnoxiously, Len's cellmate Walter interrupts their conversation "So how are you doing Pete?" Says Walter not sounding very sincere with a touch of envy in his words.

"I'm fine, thanks for asking, " answered Pete affectionately but with a hint of suspicion in his eyes. "And I'm fine too Walt, thanks for asking!" said Len, so deafening that it's a good thing that only Pete and Walter can hear him. As Pete spent the rest of the day doing all of his jobs which consisted of: rounding up the inmates for dinner, cleaning up all of the mess they had left and making sure that all the prisoners were behaving in their cells. While doing this he wondered why Walter was behaving so rudely earlier on.

As the next few days pass, Walter's rudeness spreads. Yet Pete can't figure out why. Len doesn't seem to notice this as he was too busy complaining about how much he hated the prison and how much he wanted to leave. Pete sat in the guards break room, taking a break when Walter's telepathy spoke unannounced "Hello Pete."

"Hello Walter" replied Pete "How are you?"

"Don't bother, I don't like how you have cut in between me and the only friend. It's been just us for nearly 10 years and then you come along and ruin it!"

"Wait what?" rampaged Pete furiously and full of confusion.

"You think you're so special but you're

not. I don't like that you are taking my only friend and the only person who I have trust in since my wife died!" This shocked Pete as he did not know the information just informed about Walter and he began to feel some guilt. He had no energy to continue this argument, so he disconnected from Walter's mind to end the conversation.

.

Pete went to rant about Walter to Len.

"I can't believe what Walter just did to me, he accused me of trying to steal his best friend, it's pathetic, he is nearly 60 years old and shouldn't even have a best friend! right?"

"Well I am the only person he can speak to and trust but I do see where you're coming from, we have been spending a lot of time together talking."

This annoyed Pete as he had done nothing wrong although he didn't say anything about it.

"Why didn't you mention that he lost his wife?"

"I don't know, I didn't feel it was my right too, Walter only told me after around three years of sharing a cell."

"What happened to her?"

"She was killed at a green protest around ten years ago, the same day nearly every green in this place got locked up."

"Yeah I know what you mean, it was all over the news when it happened."

"Yep, I was eleven at the time and I had just got here and I was glad to escape my good for nothing parents, they abused me all the time and to reassure myself I always said that nothing could be worse."

"My parents died when I was fifteen and by then I was in training to come here. I miss them, even if we never had the greatest bond, I would do anything to get them back."said Pete solumbly With this new found similarity, the two felt closer than ever before.

Chapter 8

Childhood Trauma

Back at the kingdom palace, Rupert

started to get more and more nervous as he began to open up about all his past trauma. He sat down in the room with Eva for a therapy session, as she is the town therapist, worried that she would judge him like his father had his whole life. He was terrified as he had always bottled all of his feelings up inside being a prince. Why would a prince, a red, have father issues it sounds stupid!

Eva waited patiently, and let Rupert take his time, getting more and more anxious as his words slowly started leaking out of his mouth. Eva said to Rupert, "You don't need to tell me everything, just tell me what's worrying you." As she could tell, Rupert doesn't want to do this, and is scared of what Eva will think. Rupert thought to himself, "Will she view me differently? " Rupert struggled to get his words out, so he took a deep breath yet still didn't have the courage to speak out about his past and childhood trauma.

Rupert got intense flashbacks, nearly crying but stopping himself from doing so, as he doesn't want to embarrass himself in front of Eva. Eva began to think to herself, what could be so servere to bring a grown man, a prince, to tears? But once he started to talk and open up about it he couldn't stop himself. The tears just came flooding out. He looked drained, his eyes soaked with tears.

Eva comforted him and reassured him that it is okay and she would help him, no judgment involved. "Rupert, all of our sessions are confidencial, I can't tell anyone anything you tell me in these sessions."

Rupert looked more relaxed and felt trust and a relationship forming between him and Eva. Feeling more comfortable and more composed, he started to open up more about his childhood and relationship between him and his father, Leo.

"My dad read me this book constantly when I was younger, it's about how life is better." Eva was really intrigued with this piece of information, what was this book? Rupert just told her there was a prehistoric book ... "Fredrick, my dad's secretary, said it was always the most top secret book but we were just children so he was probably just saying that right?"

"Yeah probably, " Eva said with caution, trying not to alarm him.

Meanwhile, Niki, one of the slaves who worked for the king, was walking past cleaning halls and overheard the mention of this so rumored book, she was anxious and scared that if this news got spread it could be damaging. If this book was released then everything could end badly.

What would Leo do?

Niki rushed to Leo, the king, anxiously as she thought she would get punished if anyone found out she knew and didn't tell anyone about it. She told Leo about the information she heard yet Leo still didn't have a reaction. He just thought it was some childs book? But was it?...

Chapter 9

There Are Eyes Everywhere

Niki and Amanda were walking down

the long and vast hallway in the middle of the palace. They had just finished the first half of their chores and were on break. Niki suggested that they should go to the library. She wanted to tell Amanda something. Amanda agreed and they made their way there. On the way Niki said, "We are so lucky to be able to be here. We're two of the few people who've been allowed here apart from the royals." Amanda smiled and admired the wonderful place around her. The palace isn't so bad, despite the fact that they were slaves and didn't get access to a lot of the rooms. At least they had places to sleep and were able to walk around whenever they wanted, as long as they didn't go near the forbidden rooms.

Finally, they reached the library. It was one of the most beautiful areas of the palace and definitely one of the biggest. The room was about twenty feet tall and fifty feet long with bookshelves traveling up and along the walls. There was a set of comfy armchairs and sofas to sit and read on with a hard wood coffee table in the centre. The floor was made of a soft and delicate red carpet to match the royals and the bookshelves look as if they were made of chocolate and the books were little sweets in comparison.

Niki heard a voice. It sounded like Rupert so she decided to go let him know that they're here. The library is like a maze so it's difficult for them to figure out where he was. On her way, she admired the books, hoping to find something interesting, however there's nothing, just history books and other boring looking ones.

Eventually, she found him. He's with a woman? Since when did Rupert have a girlfriend? Are they- "Um, excuse me? Rupert?" They're both startled and quickly move away from each other, acting like they don't know each other but she knew they did as she had recently overheard them talking about some book. "Hello Niki. Amanda too."

Amanda ran off pretending that she didn't see anything.

"Who's this?"

"None of your business. You should have no interest in who I am with. Shouldn't you be cleaning or something?"

"Sorry if we're interrupting, we're actually on break right now and wanted to uh come read a book, "

"Well I think you should leave, "

"But I'm allowed here, "

"I said get out, that's an order!"

Niki complied and looked for Amanda.

Eva and Rupert stared at each other for a while at their vibrant red and beautiful blue eyes before Rupert breaks the silence, "I'm awfully sorry about that, they're our slaves, yellows, I didn't realise it was their free time now, "

"Oh that's alright, I wanted to ask you about something, "

"I actually think you should leave now."

"What? Why?"

"I said leave."

Eva began to walk away confused but then hesitates. Why should he get to tell her what to do? Just because he's red doesn't mean he can boss her around. The reds don't seem to care about anything

but themselves, there's basically a war going on and they choose to just ignore it.
They have no real power. They're cow-
ards. She needed to say something. "You
know what, no I won't leave. I need to tell
you something, " Rupert looks confused,
he's the prince! A member of the royal
family and heir to the throne! She should
listen to him no matter what! "Did you
just say no to me?"

"Yes, I did, but please listen to me, "

"Make it quick."

"There's a rivalry between the blues and
greens right now, there was a protest not
long ago and now the blues have taken over
and have forcefully arrested most of the
greens!"

"What do you mean?"

"The blues are forcing the greens to go

to prison for no reason, you can't just sit by and not do anything, you're supposed to protect the people not let them be hurt."

"Are you sure this is happening? I'm sure Fredrick would've told my father if something was going on."

"Yes of course I'm serious! How have you not known about this?"

"We aren't allowed outside the palace, that's one of the downsides to being a royal, we all live in here, that's why we have Fredrick to tell us everything that's going on, I don't understand why he hasn't told us any of this"

"That's ridiculous, you aren't allowed to see the place you're protecting?"

"No, I wish it were different but I can't change the rules, it's been like this for generations"

"You need to go talk to the king, immediately"

"I'll go now, as should you, thank you
Eva."

Chapter 10

Uncertain Truth

Rupert walked Eva out of the library wanting answers and hurried to look for his father. He was probably in his chambers with Fredrick discussing and debating about politics, or bossing about the servants to do his everyday tasks. Rupert promptly found Leo and lectured him for answers to his plethora of questions. Leo was baffled by his normally calm son, barking confusing questions at him. Leo was so stunned by Rupert that he had no idea what to say.

There was an uncomfortable silence between them for a brief moment of time. Until Rupert calmed himself down enough to say, "Father, my therapist Eva was talking to me about some system, do you have any idea about this?" The look on Leo's face was a look of disbelief and puzzlement in what his son was saying. Was his son truly going insane?

"No, what do you mean? A system?"

Leo exclaimed. "My therapist Eva, told me a story about how life is different for greens, they're discriminated against; they're poor, most of them in prison." Rupert says with desperation. "Did you have any idea about this?" Leo was so confused and infuriated that he didn't even know what was going on in his own country, so he stormed out of his chambers and went to confront Frederick and find some answers. The politician who runs his government, if anyone would have any idea about this, it would be him. Frederick was a middle aged, relatively happy man. A tall man with a beer belly, who always had a hidden jealousy for reds. Would do anything to be one.

Leo stormed down to Frederick's office, which was in the basement of the west wing in the palace. He kicked the door open, Leo bellows, "Why didn't I know?" Frederick looked at Leo with pure confusion, "What are you talking about?" Leo had a look on his face of hatred. "The system. Why didn't I get told? I am the king, I deserve to know!" The look on Frederick's face was shocking. (He had been careful for so long). The system had been found out. Leo knew. Frederick had lost control.

Frederick understood how betrayed and angry Leo was, and wanted to explain everything. But if he did, he would have to die first. Furious, he was longing to figure out who had released the government's secret and once he did, he would have to kill them ...

Chapter 11

Gossip

After finding out about the alleged book, Eva tries to find it but she can't. This book won't defeat her and she won't be conquered. Consequently she had no luck and frustratedly went to go and ask Rupert if he knew where it might be.

"Hello I was wondering if you had any awareness of where your father has hidden that book, I have inspected all over and I don't seem to be getting anywhere?"

"Maybe it's in his chambers but good luck getting in there, it's nearly impossible."

"Thank you!"

With this information, Eva embarked to find a way into Leo's chamber. As she had suspected the door was locked but she had to keep trying. She stood still for a few minutes, hoping for an idea to pop into her head. The only sound heard was her cold, quiet breath echoing consistently. Until suddenly her eyes popped open as she had thought of a solution. Eva could use one of her paperclips from her clipboard to pick the lock. She struggled but after around five minutes, she managed to open the vast, monstrous door. The king's chambers were filled with luxurious and glamorous items. She looked in all areas, processing every cupboard but at last she found it, covered in dust and cobwebs. Eva had found the book.

She flicked through the pages, reading every single scribed word carefully. Eva couldn't keep this a secret. The pages were a brownish tint, the words were in silver cursive, it was like a book of knowledge. She went to all the local tabloids and poured out each and every undeniable truth and made it her goal to make sure that everybody knows about the system.

This invades the brains of the people who read the article written and drives them insane . Except the prisoners; it gave them hope. This newspaper article was everywhere. It distanced every household in the system including Pete's. Every morning the newspaper arrived at his doorstep around 7:00am and Pete would read every article that looked somewhat interesting or had little games hidden in the corners of the pages. Whilst he was trying to find the crossword, Pete came across this article. He scans his heterochromia eyes over the story, "The system?" he suddenly realised that this was about his life, the society that he lived in. To him that one article explained everything. This is why his mum made him wear blue a eye contact growing up and even now Reading:

"Green is the poor, the under privileged. Blue are the rich, the ones that are given a good education and a job assigned. This is why I couldn't work with animals, this is why I am a guard!"

Suddenly, Pete realises that Len and Walter wouldn't have seen the article so he rushes out of his apartment, forgetting to even say goodbye to his pet frog. His frog was a lime green tree frog called Broccoli. He loved that tiny thing with every inch of his heart. Rushing to his office, out of the corner of his eye, he sees Len and slips away from his post to go and communicate with him. Pete, earlier that morning, had stuffed the newspaper up his utility vest to be able to show Len and Walter. Through telepathy, "Read this and read it now". Len spins on his heel to face

Pete with a concerned look on his sunken, weathered face ."What are you going on about?" Len diverts his eye and pans his eyes over the article that was shoved into his face. Reading "The government categorising us through our eye colour" Walter shuffles over after being summoned by Pete, "Walter read this, the reason why you are in here is because our whole future and life revolves around our eye colour, how we are treated, our jobs and everything!" Walter realises that this could all be the source of why his wife was killed.

This sparks something inside Len and Walter, a need for change. They made a plan . . . a plan to tell anyone they could about The System'. They decided at lunch they were going to spread the article telepathically. That story spread like a rumor in a teenage locker room.

When Len and Walter spread this new gossip information, the prisoners were furious! However they had no idea what they could do. Making a change for them was going to be as difficult as well ... talking.

Chapter 12

The Turning Point

Down in the slaves quarters, Niki sat

on a crooked wooden stool reading her old and dusty book which caused her to cough and splutter. Amanda laughed, "Put that book away, you're going to make the room smell damp." Niki sat up sharply, gasping very dramatically and snapped it shut. She stood up and curtsied. "Oh sorry your majesty, can I get you anything, maybe something to soothe your sense of superiority?" She replied, sarcastically. "Anyhow, have you heard the news about Eva?" Amanda furrowed her brow and took a seat on her bunk, she patted the blanket beside her. "Sit, I need a good bit of gossip, this place is dreary most days."

"Well, " Niki began, "A little birdie told me that she gave the prisoners a book about the truth, you know before the system of contacts?"

Amanda gasped and stood, her hands used as a brush, combing through her long black locks.

Suddenly, a loud voice bellowed "Niki!" and hearing this she ran to leave the room. "See you later, get a drink of water." Amanda dragged herself up but fell back down as if chained to the bed by weights. She was having a panic attack. "Doctor, doctor!" Niki yelled as loud as she could and with that she left the room.

Niki sped down the long, winding corridor leading to Leo's royal chambers. She was out of breath, heart pounding in her chest. Calmly, she collected herself and straightened her posture. As she was about to knock Leo opened the door, he coughed. "Niki, whatever it is I would love to help but as you can see I'm kind of busy right now, I have to see to my royal duties and help my other staff members so I would appreciate it if you move out of my way please."

"Your highness." Niki whispered, raising her voice she said. "Please let me in. I need to discuss a very important matter with you." She pleaded with her eyes. He began to understand the importance of her issue. "I see. Fine you have 10 minutes, then I really do have to go. Ok?" She jumped on the chance to get into the king's good graces. "Thank you. Really, thank you, your majesty." She bravely stumbled into the heavily decorated room with golden possessions strewn everywhere. The sight was amazing to her as she had never been wealthy or been anywhere nearly as grand. As she placed herself into a plump, crimson lounge chair waiting patiently for what was about to happen. The door slammed loudly behind her as Leo sauntered over to his desk and took a seat behind it. "So, Niki, what appears to be the problem?"

"Well to be honest sir it isn't a problem for me, it's a problem for you." She muttered cautiously. "How so?" he asked with a hint of curiosity in his voice, a smile playing on his lips. "It's Eva." The smile was gone and his hands were knotted on the desk. "What do you mean it's Eva? Eva the therapist?"

Niki began to get nervous. "Yes, your highness." She stuttered. "So it appears that Eva has found a book about the truth, she has passed it through the prison and it has spread quite quickly." Leo began to appear angry. "What do you mean the truth?" He yelled, slamming his hands onto the table, knocking his ink pot everywhere. Niki stood and grabbed a cloth to mop up the spillage whilst talking to the king. "It's about life before the system, where everyone chose their destiny."

"That is it. Get out of my office now!"

They both rushed out of the office, Niki tripped on the way out but amongst the bustle of royalty and servants she didn't get helped up but briskly walked around and was left by herself. She began to weep, regretting her decision, and her tears fell onto the pearl grey marble floor. Slowly, she stood smoothing her dress and ran to the kitchen to prepare the lunch time meal.

The wind fluttered through his tousled hair, though he didn't care, all he could think about was how angry he was to have been betrayed by his favourite politician and trusted friend. Eva needs to go, he didn't care how but he needed her silenced. It's past his breaking point and he raced back to Fredrick's room. He's got some business to do.

Frederick didn't lie, he just didn't know? He made his decision and knocked three times. No one answered. Maybe Frederick already knew and was too scared. He knocked again and this time he heard some scramble to the door inside. "Leo? Hello?" He said frankly, "Ah Frederick, I need to talk to you." He replied with gritted teeth. He stepped in, looming over Frederick.

"What is the matter Leo? Can I help in some way?" The king nodded and sighed, "What do you know about this book?"

Frederick got nervous and fiddled with his thumbs a little. "Well dear Leo I've told you this before, I don't know anything about the book, it must just be a rumour. How would such a book exist without your knowledge? You are the ruler of the land so it can't have been produced without your say." He bravened. He had sweet talked Leo before so why shouldn't he be able to do it again? "Well if you're so sure Frederick, I think I've overstayed my welcome." He turned quickly on his heel and reopened the navy blue front door. "Farewell Leo, till next time." Frederick said overly happy, both parties shook hands and Leo left the house.

There were a million and one thoughts racing through his mind, he was so confused, everything in recent events has been confusing somewhat. Was Frederick lying? Or did Niki tell him this as a joke? There's no way that Eva could do this, she's just a therapist, right? And how would Eva know about the book and where could she possibly have found it? Or maybe this was all a dream? He didn't know anymore. All he wanted to do was go home and rest, to hop into his gold strewn, velvety bed and sleep all the bad things away.

Chapter 13

Eva's Ending

Bruce was one of the only people to know about life before The System, when everything was peaceful and there were no conflicts or rules between colours.He'd hoped he wouldn't have to hear about it again but that was not the case any longer.There have been stories being whispered between the guards of a book.A book that talks about a better life, a life with no restrictions or rules against what colour you are, blues being friends with greens.How do they know about the book?Bruce thought it was locked away by the king years ago and that no one could see it.It's supposed to be a secret.Who told them?

Bruce was going to get to the bottom of this mystery.He wasn't going to let the word spread.

He quickly walked by every corridor and asked every guard to walk in and out of his prison about the news. "What's this about before the system?The system has always been a thing since the world was created" This was obviously a lie but he didn't want to give them hope. "I'm not sure, apparently there's a book which tells of the world before the system, when everyone lived together peacefully, "

"Where did you hear this?" Bruce demanded, anger in his voice.

"One of the guards."

"Who?" Bruce was getting impatient now. He had already been asking people for just over two hours and had spoken to at least a hundred guards. "I can't remember, I just heard some of them talking about it whilst on break" Bruce angrily stormed off, upset that nobody knew where they had heard this story and that nobody could remember each other's names.

He had given up. Bruce began to walk

back to his office when he heard something, "-yeah Eva's story really confuses me, I can't remember hearing anything about this other life anywhere, I thought it was just this." Finally, he's found the culprit. Eva, the local therapist for the town. But how does she know? That doesn't matter, at least he knows who's told everyone. She will pay.

A door slammed open. "My king! I have important news!"

"Warden Bruce? What is it?"

"Eva, she's a traitor!"

"Eva? The therapist? What's she done now?"

"She's told everyone about the book, the one that we swore to keep a secret"

"Yes, I've heard about this already."

"You have?"

"Yes, one of my lovely servants told me earlier."

"Oh, well what are you going to do about her?"

"I haven't decided yet."

"There's not much time before it spreads, we have to punish her!"

"We aren't doing anything just yet."

"The book was sworn to be kept secret, how did she find it?"

"I don't know, I shall speak to Fredrick about this then we can make a final decision."

"But we don't have much time before everyone knows about it!"

"We will speak again soon I promise, I just need to discuss this further with Fredrick, you should leave now Bruce."

Bruce leaves, not daring to challenge

the king's opinion. He orders the guards to escort Eva to his office as soon as she is seen, immediately!

Within twelve hours Eva was escorted by two guards to Bruce's office. Bruce swiveled in his chair, a stern expression on his face. "Eva, you are being arrested and taken to king Leo for copying and releasing top secret texts into the public."

"What? They deserve to know! Most of the guards don't even like it here!"

"Nonsense! You two, " He looked at the two guards holding Eva, "do you like working here?"

They both glanced at each other, frightened, then looked back at the warden, "Yes, sir" they stuttered. "See? They're fine!"

"Whatever, they just don't want to get fired!"

"Guards, escort this traitor to the king's palace, I will tell him about your arrival."

"Yes sir."

The two guards forcefully dragged Eva out of the room as she struggled and squirmed.

There was a loud knock on the door. The door opened and the king stood there waiting for Eva's arrival.He didn't look happy. "Thank you both, you can leave now." The guards bowed and walked away. "Now, you, join me in my office." Eva could've ran away but didn't dare because she knows that the warden will only hunt her down again. The walk to Leo's office felt like the longest walk of her life, though it only took 5 minutes. She constantly darted her eyes around to try and look for Rupert, hoping he would help her. He never showed up. She felt betrayal and sorrow as she thought

Rupert would be the one to follow through but when he didn't, sadness came.

Leo opened the office door and sat down at his desk beside Fredrick. He motioned for Eva to sit down opposite him and she hastily did. "Now, I've heard that you've stolen and copied top secret property of the royals and shared it with the public. Is this true?"

"Yes, I did, my lord.They deserve to know! Do you not understand there is a literal war going on, many people are in danger!"

"I trust Fredrick with my life, he helps me make all of my decisions and makes sure my family is safe, if he says nothing bad is going on then I trust his word."

"I refuse to accept this! He's lying to you!" Eva was furious about how clueless the king really was. "Silence! I trust Fredrick with my life there's no way he could be lying!" Frederick begins to smile, "Thank you, Leo. Now, what should we do with her?"

"I don't want to do this Eva, but I have no choice. Eva Marshall, you have stolen and copied top secret royal property therefore I sentence you, " there was a long pause and a slight hesitation, "to an execution."

"WHAT? No! You can't! This is outrageous! They deserve to know!"

"I'm sorry Eva but this is the conclusion me and Fredrick came to." There was a deafening silence in the room. Eva now shook with fear, thought to herself, "I'm going to die . . . I'm going to die . . . " She continued to tell herself this yet it didn't change the unrealty.

Chapter 14

Lost Love

Eva trembled as she was led to the guillotine, her hands shackled together. To
make matters worse, guards were banging

on the gates yelling but she couldn't make it out. She felt a sudden sullenness in her heart as she got nearer and saw her lover and his father stood side by side next to what would be her murderer. "Why him?" She thought, "He's supposed to love me to want to keep me safe, but no. The traitor is here to watch me die. Well I hope he's happy. All over that wretched no good book, it's probably better this way anyway. Why would I ever think him and his family were good people? I'm such a fool."

"Get Eva! Get Eva!!" the guards yelled, the only thing to break the melancholy silence. "No." Frederick, said to whomever was fetching her, "She stays here and that is an order, got it?" His voice was threatening as if daring the poor guy to disobey. The guard shuddered and took a step back

and offered her to him and pushed her for-
ward. As she attempted to steady herself, her trembling knees gave way beneath
her and she slumped onto the floor. Eva
glanced up at Rupert and he gave her such
a morose, I'm sorry look with his deep
blood red eyes. Whilst he thought no one
was watching Frederick gave Eva a swift
kick to the chest causing her to lay sprawled
on the floor. She heard the congregation
gasp loudly with displeasure. Her chest
hurt so bad she could feel it begin to bruise
but she stood her ground and didn't let the
tears fall down her face. She couldn't let
him know he'd hurt her.

"Come on Leo, It's the right thing to
do, she's betrayed you and the civilians of
this country. You know that The System is
needed and it's always been this way." He

hissed, spewing his harsh words into Leo's ear like the dreaded snake he was. "Come on Leo, we need to do this. Just imagine what other lies she could spread, she could cause a rebellion or another protest? Remember the last one?"

"Hush" Leo demanded. "I'm thinking." They stood for a while, her impatience clung to her as she wondered if she would live to see tomorrow or if he would behead her. Leo wouldn't do that to her would he? She had been his therapist for years now and he had opened up to her about his deepest secrets and what he feared in life. Is it because she knew too much or he knew too little? "Kill me then." She spat at him, he could feel the outrage radiating around those three words. He looked puzzled, contemplating life or death. She stood and yelled "Do it!"

"Father no, please don't do this, I'm begging you I love her!" Rupert cried. "Father, please, please." He dropped to his knees and shook his head. "What needs to be done has to be done, you will learn this when you are king. However she needs to die, she has done more than enough for this kingdom and now her time has come now to step out of my way." he said coldly and pushed through him, as if he was a ghost. "Please" Rupert whispered once more, though he got ignored. "Be quiet, your father is saving everyone from her lies Rupert, you're such a headache." He shook his head. It was as if Rupert's voice was gone.

"It's time Leo come on, you need to do this not only for yourself but for every-

one who looks up to you as their leader."
Leo grabbed Eva wrists and yanked her
away from where she stood viciously in
front of him."You! Here, now!" He demanded tones of indignation in his words.
Eva stood strong and looked the king in
his bittersweet eyes.

Rupert's mouth dropped and Eva kneeled
before the chopping block, her curly, chocolate brown hair fell onto her face. "Now
come on, Frederick, we're waiting, she needs
to go."

"On the 6th of October 3021 Eva Marshall is due to be beheaded." Leo shouted.
A single tear rolled down Eva's cheek while
Frederick watched with glee. It was time.
It was all over. Leo grabbed the rope at
the side of the guillotine and pulled, lifting
the articulating blade to its highest point.

A lump had risen in Rupert's throat, his legs began to quiver. Oh how he would miss her so. He would never forgive his wretched father for this. "Three, two, one!" Leo let go of the rope and the blade fell. It hit Eva's neck with such brute force, Eva was dead. Blood squirted from her neck splurging all over the trio's faces like a fountain. Her head rolled to the side and she stared at Rupert, making a lot of eye contact. "I love you, Eva." Tears fell one after another and didn't stop. Leo grabbed him by the collar and jerked him away. She looked so pale and lifeless. Rupert stood puffing out his chest like a ferocious beast, he put in all of his strength by hitting his fathers face. "You murderer! You killed the only woman I loved!" He yelled loudly. He ran out of the gates and

up the palace steps leaving his father behind and stood with Frederick. "What have
I done?" Leo thought to himself.

Chapter 15

The Plan

Furious about what happened to Eva, Rupert made his way to the prison. Despite not knowing what he was going to do, he was determined to go there just to see if this place was the same as eva had described it to him during their sessions.

After hearing about the system, Rupert decided that he must set the greens free as he knew that they were wrongfully imprisoned because of the rules in society. For most of his life Rupert believed in the world as he thought that it was always like that and that it was right but he finally learned the truth, that the world is corrupt and needed changing and he wanted to help change it.

When Rupert made it to the huge steel prison doors he was shocked to see how appalling it looked. The walls were covered in moss and what looked like moldy food possibly thrown by one of the inmates. The building itself was made of concrete 1 and it looked clean from the outside but inside was completely different. This place made Rupert feel guilty for the prisoners but also happy that he gets to live in a luxurious palace.

Rupert, still furious, strutted into the prison and demanded to see the warden and as he marched through the door the atmosphere suddenly turned cold and even Rupert was intimidated but he stood strong and went on with his plan.

"I demand you to let the prisoners go at once!" demanded Rupert looking furious

Bruce, slightly startled, replied saying, "I don't think I will, you are not my king or my superior so you do not give me orders."

This infuriated Rupert as he was a royal and even if he isn't the king he believed that he should still have respect.

"Listen here you will do what I say!" roared Rupert angrier than ever. This made Bruce furious and all of a sudden he upper cutted Rupert knocking him down to the ground unconscious.

When Rupert woke up he saw nothing but darkness. At first he assumed it was just night but when he looked around at the surroundings closely he saw that he was in one of the prison cells. He also realised that his face was swollen from where he had been viciously attacked.

It took him about an hour before he fully regained consciousness and remembered his mission.

He had to think of a way to get out of the cell and to free the other inmates, but how?

Suddenly a guard showed up, it was

Pete.

Pete recognised him immediately and couldn't help but say hello.

"Hey you, guard, I order you to let me out of here at once. I have something urgent to do."

But shockingly Pete listens and lets him out.

"Thank you, I need to get the greens out of here they are innocent and and."

But suddenly Pete interrupted him and said, "I know, the therapist, Eva, released a story that explained everything and I want to help, I am half green and my friend Len is green and I can't find him. I was on my way to his cell."

"Ok, this is strange but I'm glad you're here I guess so let's go."

With that they set off to free the others. As they were letting the others out they had run into a problem, they didn't know what to do as they had no way to speak because Rupert couldn't speak to them and Pete is still trying to get used to his telepathy and like Len and Walter, they were daydreaming and couldn't seem to hear them normally. But as if it were a miracle Len had come running down the corridor. He then explained that he had been with the warden and he had left Walter alone in the cell.

"Well that's ok we were about to go let everyone out" explained both Pete and Rupert simultaneously.

"Well stop, it's almost ten anyway so the doors will open on their own, we should probably focus on telling the others that we are planning to set them free." This didn't occur to Pete but he did agree so they waited until ten, which felt like it was hours away and when it arrived Len used his telepathy to tell everyone about the plan, this seemed to tire him out as after he did it he looked like a ghost. But it seemed to work as all of the inmates came out of their cells and Pete could hear all of their excitement as they set off to escape the prison.

Chapter 16

The Sacrifice

The charcoal corridor was Walters run-
way. His long strides brought him closer
and closer to Bruce's office. Walter pounded

on the titanium door between him and the rest of his life. It cautiously opens. Standing there was Bruce, a small, muscly, angry excuse for a man. "You murdered my wife." Walter sends telepathically, forwell knowing that Bruce cannot hear him. Walter sighs through the grit of his teeth. Bruce stands in the doorway, his unit of a body blocking any space to get through, "Go back to your cell greenie and let it go!"

Walter uppercuted Bruce using every single ounce of his old body to hurt Bruce. He should hurt, he should feel pain. Walter wanted Bruce to suffer like his wife did. A life for a life. Bruce was startled not expecting a hit from Walter himself. Plunging for the gun in Bruce's utility belt, Walter stumbled into the startled officer, starting a fight. Bruce screamed for assistance.

No one came, he's doomed. Walter stole-
Bruce's gun and pinned him to the floor
with his foot.This new found strength is
just out of pure adrenaline. Bang: right
between the eyes. Bang (one more for good
look) his blood was blown all over the floor
in a crimson mess. Bruce is dead! Walter didn't realise that everyone had seen
him, the whole prison some looked startled, some looked happy but all Walter
cared about was Len who just looked relieved to see him.

The alarms sounded. This was it they
were coming for him but he didn't care.
Bruce was dead, his wife was avenged. All
that mattered to Walter now is letting everyone else run free. There was a plan that
he and Len spoke about in their cell one
night. It was just an idea, however it could

work. All the guards were on their way to Walter now. If Walter could distract the guards long enough for the other prisoners to escape, that would save a lot of lives. He could sacrifice himself? That was exactly what he was going to do.

Walter could hear the heavy shuffle of footsteps along the corridor. Coming for him. To kill him, he wasn't ready to die yet. He wanted to see this so-called perfect world that everybody talks about. He was a book with one more chapter left but this was the end of the road for him.

The guards bursted into the room, flooding around Walter. Precariously, stepping over the warden's stiff body on the floor. They started yelling at him, firing digging insults at him, cutting him apart from the inside out. Walter took a blow to the back of his head making his brain physically shake inside his aged skull. Everything stopped, it went blank.

Walter was gone, dead, free to go join his wife. The inmates took the dreaded sound of Walter's death to start the revolution. He died so they could be free. A sacrifice. Pete saw for the first time that Len was crying. Pete felt guilty as he and Walter never reconciled, but he appreciated his sacrifice and knew what had to be done.

Chapter 17

Freedom

The prisoners scurried to start a new life. A stampede rushing to freedom. Adrenaline kicked in as prisoners bolted to a normal reality. The hope of a new life without the system urged them to dash quicker. The sound of scampering feet travelled through the walls of the system, the walls now having no presence or sense of belonging, left nothing but a drained building.

A single soul remained, uncertain of what to do. Amanda, a young 19 year old servant with mental health issues, working for the royal family remained humble. Aghast of the real world, struggled with the decision to hasten. Becoming responsible and yearning for freedom. The castle and her yellow assignment was all she knew. How does she live life normally when this was her normality?

Amanda makes the confrontation to spurt after stepping up to herself and gaining confidence after seeking the brave greens leading the way. She felt pressured into leaving and was frightened considering this was the only world she knew. Almost mollycoddled in the past, she now opens a new chapter having to look after herself as she chooses to make her own verdicts. No more living in secret, no more imprisonment.

uld be pointless, since it was so silent but to the telepathic it was a momentous occasion.

To an outsider this rebellion would be pointless, since it was so silent but to the telepathic it was a momentous occasion. They have the whole future ahead of them and it looks bright, beautiful and bewildered. From dark to light and hot to cold. Children could play and wouldn't have a limit. Parents could watch and enjoy the sight of happiness spread across their children's faces. Everyone could communicate telepathically and have conversations with their loved ones. Jobs people actually wanted to do and a life they could choose for themselves, their own paths for their own futures instead of some messed up ancient law doing it for them.

Trust isn't easy to gain when mixing with people from the real world, it will take a while for them to appreciate the greens skills and convey that level of trust on our behalf. The doors were wide open and a sense of fear still stood within the limits of freedom but this is the new story, this is the new chapter, children look back and see this system as an error in society but to them it was a reality. It will always stay with t

Chapter 18

The Coronation

After lots of thought in desperation, Leo abdicated from the throne in recognition of the kingdom. He knew that the next in line was his only son, Rupert, and he was very adequate for the throne because he was well educated on the kingdom and system. And the greens started a new life and Pete and Len are happy that they can be free.

With pride and persistence, Rupert took the throne, knowing he will be an obedient king and will overthrow the system rules. He reminisced over Eva, wishing that she was sitting next to him as his queen. He's commissioned a painting of her to be put on the wall next to the throne. After all, it's because of her that he's now allowed out of the palace and that he's now king.

His first decree was for Frederick to be imprisoned for his substandard actions and the response given from him was an instant regret for what he did. Although he still felt no remorse towards his attitude, he was silenced. And now that Rupert knew about the system, he banished all the rules so that everyone could live a better life, like in the olden times.

Actions speak louder than words in this case as Frederick's words were also taken from him in a karma, revenge like way. Frederick, now suppressed and shellshock, was left solitary in a cell with only his thoughts as company. He would sit his days in a ghastly, secluded corner regretting his past intentions. No contact driving him to an extreme level of abandonment and rejection.

Leo, now content that someone superior will finally rule the kingdom, is at peace with his settlement .

As for the outside world, Pete now lives

with Len and his frog, Broccoli, and there was a statue made to remember Walter and his sacrifice. This made Len incredibly cheery but also sad. Fortunately, Niki was released from her position and Amanda, who seemed rather content, remained a servant working for Rupert but she was now allowed outside and paid. Everything was how it should be...

Or was it?

.

THE END

Our Authors

Eve Irving

Hi, I am 14 years old and I am a dancer. I was very skeptical about the whole situation at the beginning. My English teacher told me to give it a go and it ended up being really fun.I developed the character Eva Marshal .This book is everything that me and my peers expected it to be and we all had a really fun time writing it xo

Victoria Kaczmarczyk

Hi, my name is Vic, I am 14 years old. I wasn't sure I'd like writing a book but it has been fun. My english teacher encouraged me to do this and it has been a good experience. The character that I developed is Amanda and I'm happy how the book turned out, we all developed more skills during this book writing :)

Amy Parker

Helloo, my name is Amy and I'm 14 years old and in year 10. I live in England with my mum, dad and 2 brothers, Ben and Matthew. My best friends are Korbyn Wood (he's one of the other authors of this book) and Jordan Byrne. I like to watch YouTube and Twitch and I play Minecraft. I also like to draw and listen to music, my favourite band is Lovejoy. I really love animals, I've always wanted a dog or cat but sadly we can't have one. I want to do animal management at college and hopefully work in a zoo when I'm older and maybe try streaming as a hobby in the future. I'm really happy with this book and I think everyone did really well and I hope you enjoyed it as much as we did writing it, my character was Niki :D

Korbyn Wood

Hello, my name is Korbyn and I am 14 years old and I live in England. I like to draw and I do karate. I have three dogs, a husky who is called Demon but I call him Sausage and I have a king charles called Klaus and a German shepherd named Bear who is very cute and my best friend Amy loves them. I love animals, mainly dogs and frogs and one day I wish to work with them. My favourite shows are Modern Family, Big bang theory and Brooklyn Nine Nine. I also enjoy films like Hunger Games and watching all of this has given me an immense imagination that has come across in this novel so I hope you enjoy the characters and story and I especially hope you enjoy my character Pete and I hope you despise my friend Charlotte's character Walter. ;D

Charlotte Cooke

Hello, my name is Charlotte, aka Walter in the book, and I am 14 years old. Writing this book developed a lot of confidence and I would definitely write another if I had the chance. Before I started year 10, I wasn't very good in English but I had an opportunity being put into Mrs Rankin's class and with a good teacher I improved massively. Writing this book was NOT easy but it IS when you're not the only one and have the support given. As well as liking English, I also find comfort in music and like to play the piano in my spare time. Writing a book also relieves a lot of stress and is a very calming activity. I had fun experiencing being a real life author and made a new friend (Korbyn). I hope you will enjoy reading this book as much as I enjoyed writing it :) x

Morgan Davidson

Hello, my name is Morgan, I'm 14 years old and I helped write Frederick in the book. Whilst writing this story I have developed confidence in my linguistic skills. Before I started Year 10 I wasn't very happy with the quantity or quality of the work I produced, but being in Miss Johnson's class and the compliments on my writing from various staff members, I believe I have improved. Writing 'The System' has been a great experience not just for me but for my peers alike. I'd say if I had another chance to write a book I would definitely take it. However, other than looking at English, I really enjoy drawing and painting, especially water colours! It feels amazing being an accomplished author. I hope you enjoyed our story as much as I enjoyed writing it and thank you for reading.

Jacob Cliffe

Hi my name is Jacob and I'm 14 years old. I found writing this book difficult but it was worth it in the end .I play football and watch it most weekends as I have a season ticket at Everton.

Kyla Gater

Hi, my name is Kyla and im 14 years old, thank you for reading our book. This experience has been so fun and educational as I have learnt lots of new skills. We each developed our own characters in this book and I developed Leonard, he was so fun to create and I'm happy with the way he turned out.

Printed in Great Britain
by Amazon

71945572R00081